The Shift

Todd F. Cope

ISBN 0-9663413-0-9

Todd F. Cope
Spanish Fork, Utah

For speaking engagements please call
(801) 798-7891

Out of the mouth of babes...

Psalms 8:2

For all the teachers in my life

1

"Jefferson County Hospital, this is Oakville Ambulance." The voice from the radio caught me off guard. I left the desk where I was trying to finish the charting from a busy Friday evening. Inside the ambulance communication room, I adjusted the volume on the receiver.

"Go ahead Oakville," I responded into the microphone.

"Jefferson, we are en route to your facility with a 76-year-old female patient complaining of severe, crushing chest pain."

The words "chest pain" always seem to get the attention of the entire Emergency Room Staff, which that night consisted of Dr. Larry Zobell, Michelle, the receptionist and me. Dr. Zobell leaned around the corner to listen in on the conversation. He had the reputation of being the best emergency room physician in the county, so his presence was reassuring.

The voice from the radio continued. "She has been experiencing the pain for approximately four hours. Respirations are shallow and rapid at approximately 30 per minute; we have her on O_2. Her pulse is 84 and irregular, B.P. is 100 over 54. We've been unable to establish an I.V. at this point. She is on the monitor, and we can send you a strip if you want. Our E.T.A. is approximately five minutes."

"Have them give nitro, and let me see the strip," Dr. Zobell said as he returned to the dictation he had interrupted.

Acknowledging his orders, I returned to the handset. "Oakville, go ahead with the strip, and give 0.4 mg nitro glycerine sublingual. We'll advise of any other orders after reviewing the strip. Jefferson County Clear."

I switched on the printer and shook my head as I saw the potentially unstable cardiac rhythm sent by the ambulance monitor.

"I'll call for back up," I said, handing the strip to Dr. Zobell.

After asking Michelle to page the night supervisor, I went to work preparing the cardiac room for our soon-to-arrive guest. It was the largest room in the emergency center and always seemed bleak and cold. Its array of open shelves was stuffed with emergency medications and stainless steel instruments. Gauges, monitors and receptacles dotted the back wall. The large overhead surgical light gave it an almost mechanical **appearance.** **Positioned** in the center of the room was the narrow bed. I raised it to the appropriate height, then lowered the foot slightly to match the usual slope of an ambulance gurney. With the defibrillator cart handy and the cardiac monitor on, I headed outside to wait.

The cool April breeze seemed to invigorate me as I stood outside watching for the ambulance. Over the hill to the east, I could see the red glow of flashing lights. My mind began to race as I rehearsed the chest pain protocol. I had been here many times before and still never knew what to expect. The ambulance arrived, and I opened the back doors to help lift the gurney down. There in front of me was a slender figure, drenched with perspiration. Strings of long grey hair were matted to her pale face. The oxygen mask made it even more difficult to imagine her usual appearance, yet somehow, there was something familiar about this woman. I interrogated the Ambulance Crew as we wheeled the patient into the emergency room.

"Any changes along the way?" I asked.

"No, and the nitro didn't help," Stephen replied. "Sorry we didn't get the I.V. in, but you know how it is when these veins clamp down."

Stephen was a veteran member of the Oakville volunteer crew. I had watched his skills during the previous five years and knew there was no need for an apology. Even under the best of circumstances, starting an I.V. in the back of a moving ambulance is like trying to thread a needle while riding a horse.

"No problem," I said, turning my attention to the patient. "What's your name?" I asked as Stephen and his fellow volunteers helped me move her from the ambulance gurney to the E.R. bed. The question was as much to satisfy my curiosity as it was for hospital records. I was sure I knew this person.

"Jenny," was the muffled reply from behind the oxygen mask.

"Well Jenny," I began my usual introduction, "my name is Blake, and I'll be taking care of you. I'm going to ask you some questions, and the answers will help us determine how we can make you feel better, okay?"

"Okay," she responded. Her words said she was all right, but I could sense fear in her voice, in spite of my reassurance.

My full intention was to begin with the customary battery of questions associated with her symptoms, but for some reason I blurted out, "Do I know you?"

Before she had time to respond to my outburst, Dr. Zobell came into the room. He rescued her from my inquisitiveness by asking the appropriate questions. I listened intently, while continuing with my other tasks, hoping to glean some information that would help me figure out who she was. I held her slender hand in mine as I placed an I.V. catheter into her left arm. When the doctor asked about life at home, she expressed her loneliness since the death of her husband eight years before. She folded her thumb across the palm of her hand and stroked the band of the beautiful diamond on her ring finger. She spoke tenderly of their fifty years together.

By this time Martha Nelson, the night supervisor, had joined us in the room. She handed me some morphine to give through the I.V. line and prepared to do an EKG. The medication did little to decrease the pain.

"Do you work?" Dr. Zobell asked.

"I'm a retired teacher," Jenny replied.

That was just enough information to spark my memory. Interrupting the doctor, I said with anticipation, "Mrs. Curtis."

"That's right," Jenny said as she gritted her teeth at the increasing pain.

"You taught me in eighth grade. You were my type teacher," I said with almost inappropriate enthusiasm.

A smile came over her face as she responded, "Yes, I believe I did; you're the Thomas boy, aren't you?"

"You remember me then?" I asked.

"Of course I do," she said.

Suddenly, as if I had forgotten where I was, I began accessing memories that would help renew an old friendship.

"It's been so many years," I said. There was no response to my statement.

"It's still hurting," Jenny groaned through clenched teeth.

I administered more morphine in another attempt to ease her pain.

Though I had often cared for people I knew, this time was somehow different. I felt a real need to help this woman who had once been an important part of my life.

The EKG showed severe and progressing injury to Jenny's heart, so Dr. Zobell had me mixing a virtual pharmacy of drugs. I continued thinking of my days as a student at Oakville Junior High School so many years ago.

When I returned to Jenny's bedside, fear overwhelmed me. Her face was ashen grey, and the heart monitor displayed a rhythm that commonly precedes cardiac arrest. I had seen this combination before and began to feel sick inside.

"How are you feeling now Mrs. Curtis?" I asked as though I expected a positive response. I could barely make out her words, but I did not dare remove the oxygen mask. I moved my head so my ear was next to her face.

I thought I heard her say, "Remember the shift key."

"I'm sorry," I said, "I didn't quite hear you."

This time, her words were clear. "Remember the shift key."

Before I had time to contemplate what she had said, the cardiac monitor began to alarm.

"Dr. Zobell, she's in V-Fib," I yelled as I placed two gel pads on her chest and grabbed the defibrillator. The doctor confirmed my reading and nodded his approval to shock her.

"Charged, 200 joules, clear!" I said as I sent a jolt of electricity through her heart. Her body twitched, but the rhythm did not change.

"I'm going again, charged 300 joules, clear!" I repeated as I once again applied firm pressure to the paddles against Jenny's skin and pushed the discharge buttons. The irregular waves continued to march across the oscilloscope screen as if daring me to regulate them.

Angrily I charged the defibrillator to 360 joules and shouted, "clear!" as my trembling thumbs depressed the buttons on top of the paddles. Jenny's body jerked like someone who had just been frightened out of a deep sleep and the rhythm on the monitor changed.

"Asystole, Martha, push the atropine and epi.," Dr.

Zobell said as he looked at the monitor and then at Jenny.

I felt as if he had given the last order simply to make me feel better. I reached over and took the syringes from Martha's hand. Injecting the medications, I watched the monitor, knowing the battle was probably over with death as the victor. The steady straight line continued to divide the monitor screen.

"Anyone have any other ideas before I call it?" Dr. Zobell asked.

Advanced life support procedures flooded my mind, but none of them appropriate for the circumstances.

Dr. Zobell broke the silence. "Put 2248 hours as the time of death."

2

"Are you all right Blake?" Martha put her hand on my shoulder as if she anticipated my answer.

"I'm fine, why?" I asked as if I did not know.

"You don't usually take this long for postmortem care," she responded.

To look at her, you would think Martha was one of those head nurses we were warned about in nursing school. Her long grey hair was always put up in a bun, and she always wore a white dress. White shoes and nylons that rubbed together when she walked completed the stereotype. She was affectionately referred to by others in the hospital as "Sarge," but I liked Martha. Her dry wit always seemed to get a laugh out of me, but it was her kind heart that really won me over.

I looked at the clock and asked, "What do you mean?" before realizing it had been twenty minutes and I had not even turned off the monitor.

"What can I do to help?" she asked as she began picking up medication wrappers and needle caps

9

from the floor.

"I've done this a hundred times," I said without regard to her last question, "but I just can't get it out of my mind."

Martha looked a bit puzzled. "Get what out of your mind?"

"Her comment, I'm not sure if she really meant it or was just delirious." I continued. "If she did mean it, what did she mean? She said she remembered me. Do you think she was talking to me? She was probably just delirious, huh?"

"What are you talking about?" Martha asked, trying not to laugh.

"Mrs. Curtis. Just before she arrested, she said to remember the shift key. Normally I would just dismiss it, but she said it twice. This probably sounds stupid, but I think she was trying to tell me something."

Martha continued cleaning up the mess. "I'll leave the monitor leads and I.V. for you," she said as she turned the monitor off. She sat on the stainless steel stool and just looked at me.

"Martha, do you think it's stupid?" I asked.

"She was obviously speaking to you, but I don't know what she meant. You're sure that's what she said?"

"I'm positive," I replied almost defensively. "I even had her repeat it."

THE SHIFT

Martha stood up and looked me in the eye. "Blake, there's one thing I've learned in my thirty years of nursing: When a patient that close to death speaks, they usually have something important to say. You'd be wise to figure out what she meant."

With that, Martha took a face cloth from the shelf above the sink, wet it and handed it to me before leaving the room.

"Thanks," I said, too late for her to hear.

I took the monitor leads and defibrillator pads off Jenny's chest and wiped her face with the moist cloth. After removing the I.V. catheter, I placed a blanket over her torso and legs. Somehow, I could not bring myself to cover her face as I usually would have done.

"Michelle tells me you have no family Mrs. Curtis, but I'll be sure someone from your neighborhood or church is contacted so proper funeral arrangements can be made." My words seemed to echo in the once again bleak room, but it did not seem cold right then.

I was not one to talk to the dead, though I had been known to talk to myself. But I was not talking to myself, and I do not believe I was talking to the dead. It does not take long to develop a belief in life after death when you regularly witness people of all ages dying under a variety of circumstances. The always familiar feeling confirmed for me that I was talking to Jenny, who was still alive, just in another place. Even with this belief intact, I felt lonely. The whole world should have stopped and experienced the pain with me, or at least allowed me the pleasure of uninterrupted self pity.

I returned to the nurse's station, got a Death Notice form from the filing cabinet and began filling it out. "Michelle, do you have a chart ready on Mrs. Curtis?"

"I don't have enough information to even enter her in the computer," she called from the reception area. "Martha said you knew her and could probably help."

"I used to know her," I mumbled as I picked up the ambulance report and walked back to Michelle's desk. I handed her the paper. "All I know is her name and the town she lived in, but you should be able to get some good information from this. Let me know when you've got it, and I'll call someone about what to do with her."

My last statement could seem somewhat heartless to those unfamiliar with an E.R. nurse's natural defense mechanism of blocking emotions. This time, my words sounded cold even to me. I found myself consciously avoiding memories of the days as a student in Jenny's type class. Perhaps not prepared for what a stroll down "memory lane" might reveal, I kept telling myself I did not have time to deal with the past right then. After all, I needed to finish my shift.

Back at the desk, I began looking for a telephone directory. Michelle soon joined me.

"So what do you do in a case like this?" she asked, handing me a still practically blank Patient Information Sheet. She had been unable to gather any additional information about Jenny. The ambulance report only confirmed what we already knew: There was no identified next-of-kin, no emergency contact name and no insurance carrier.

"Normally," I said, "I'd contact the mortuary to come get the body and then tell them to contact the police."

"What do you mean, normally?" she questioned.

Michelle had only been working at the hospital for a short time. Unlike most who filled the high turnover night shift position, she was there by choice. As a nursing student, she gained valuable exposure to her chosen career. We often talked when the nights were slow and had developed a kind of brother-sister relationship, without the sibling rivalry. Though young and inexperienced, the questions sprouting from her curiosity usually challenged my thinking.

"I guess I mean this time isn't normal," I replied.

"Then it makes a difference because you know her?" she asked sincerely.

"Only to me, I suppose." My response would have been sufficient for most people, but I knew Michelle's inquisitive mind would not rest until she understood what I meant. I continued. "I couldn't feel right about turning her over to someone else. All the police ever have time for is a superficial investigation that rarely brings any additional information to light. The deceased is then placed under the jurisdiction of the County Attorney. Mrs. Curtis would be put in a pine box and placed in the ground, a small brass plaque with her name and death date being her only epitaph. She deserves better."

Michelle contemplated my words. "She must have been pretty special to you Blake. Anyone would think she was a long lost relative the way you're handling things."

"Michelle," I asked, "what did Martha say about me and Mrs. Curtis?"

"Nothing, just that you knew her and would make the necessary arrangements," she replied.

I nodded in approval and continued my search for the directory. I telephoned the only mortuary in Oakville and arranged for them to come get Jenny. When they asked for her family information, I told them they would be contacted tomorrow by someone who could answer their questions.

While waiting for someone from the mortuary, I tried

THE SHIFT

to prioritize my, already busy, Saturday schedule. It quickly became evident that Jenny, and the Easter egg hunt I had promised my children, would have to rank higher on my list than sleep.

Usually, when the attendant from the mortuary came to pick up a body, I was happy to let him work on his own. That night, I met him outside and accompanied him to the room where Jenny lay as though resting peacefully. There was no talking as we put her on a stretcher, similar to the one on which she arrived. As we wheeled her through the emergency center and out to the awaiting van, I thought about the contrast between Jenny's departure and her arrival only a few hours earlier. She came accompanied by flashing lights and escorted by three strong men, each doing what they could to make her feel better. She left in a dark grey minivan, with decorative chrome landau bars where windows should have been, and no one was attempting to change a thing.

"I'll see you later Mrs. Curtis," I said. I closed the back door of the van and watched it pull from under the canopy and onto the highway.

3

"I'll see you later Mrs. Curtis." The words echoed through my mind as I turned out the lights in the room where Jenny had taken her last breath. The seemingly inherent chill had returned, encouraging my rapid departure. I walked back and sat at the desk where I had been working.

Part of me wanted to talk to someone and I knew Michelle would be a willing listener. But, I resigned myself to the fact that I needed time to sort through my feelings. Jenny's final words sparked something inside me, and I was determined to fan and encourage that spark until its meaning burned bright and clear in my mind.

Though there were several hours remaining until the end of my shift, the emergency room was quiet. Dr. Zobell had retired to the doctor's sleep room, Michelle was busy at the computer, and I had finished my charting.

"I'll be in the back," I called out to Michelle as I made my way down the short, dimly lit hallway. I retreated to the room identified by the sign on the wall as the Nurse's

17

Lounge. It was really no more than a closet, just big enough for a reclining chair and a table supporting a small microwave oven. The narrow passage would have been taken up by the footrest if anyone actually reclined in the chair. Still, it was a peaceful haven for a tired nurse and his self administered debriefing.

I sat in the chair and began thinking about Junior High School and the day I first met Jenny.

As I sat at the grey typewriter, I noticed something was wrong. There was no electrical cord and the keys had no letters on them.

"How do they expect us to learn to type on these old things?" I said to the girl sitting in front of me. She just glanced at me from the corner of her eye and acted as if she had not heard my question.

I was used to being ignored. Although we were not poor, my parents worked hard just to meet our basic needs. Unfortunately, their definition of "needs" did not always agree with mine. Now that I was in Junior High, I felt I needed the right brand of clothing to be part of the group. After all, it was the 1970's. Sadly for me, without designer jeans and name brand gym shoes, the only thing I was part of was the class of Junior High students known as "Geeks." I am sure the calculator case on my belt and pocket protector in my front pocket did not help my image in the eyes of my peers. The only thing I lacked was black rim glasses; then I could have been the Poster Child for Geeks everywhere.

My only friends were my three older brothers, the youngest of which was seven years older than I. We seldom did things together, except at home. If not for the fact that my brothers were still remembered as star athletes at Oakville High, I would have been a regular, though unwilling, sparring partner for every bully in town. I think the only reason I enrolled in a type class was I knew it would be full of girls and they would be less likely to pick on me.

I was not sure what to think of the lady who sat at the front of the classroom. I assumed she was the teacher. She soon introduced herself as Mrs. Curtis, explained the class rules and proceeded to show us some finger exercises on the typewriter. As the rhythmic clicking began, she circulated through the room to see how everyone was doing.

"You seem to have a knack for typing. Have you had training before?" asked Mrs. Curtis. She had stopped by my desk and was looking over my shoulder.

"Nope," I replied. I do not know how I could have shown any kind of promise on the first day of class. The only thing any of us had typed was "a;sldkfjghfjdksla;" about a hundred times. Still, her comment made me feel at ease in her classroom. I decided I was going to like it there.

Each day as I sat pecking away at the typewriter keys, Mrs. Curtis came by my desk and made some kind of positive remark about my skills. I soon realized that she seldom commented to any of the other students. I was not sure why she had taken such an interest in me, but the reason was not important. For the first time in my life, someone outside my family seemed to like me.

"How was your shift?" Pat asked interrupting my reverie.

"Busy until about midnight," I replied.

"Do you have anything planned for today besides sleep?" she asked.

Pat had worked the shift that followed mine since I began my employment in the emergency room. She was always checking to see if I was "taking care" of myself. I think she was more concerned that I would return to relieve her Sunday night than she was about the state of my health.

"Except for an Easter egg hunt, I didn't, at least not until a few hours ago," I responded.

THE SHIFT

"So now what's up?" she asked.

"I guess I'm planning a funeral," I replied, hoping she would not ask any more questions, but knowing she would.

"I'm sorry, I didn't realize." She continued. "Is it for a family member?"

"No, just an old friend, sort of," I said.

"You're planning a funeral for someone who is sort of an old friend?" she asked curiously. "How did you get involved in something like that, and on Easter weekend?"

"Just lucky I guess," I said, then quickly changed the subject. "There's no one here, so I don't really have anything to report. See you tomorrow night." I picked up my coat and left the lounge.

"Yeah," Pat responded in surprise to my obvious desire to leave, "and Happy Easter."

I drove into my driveway fifteen minutes later and suddenly wondered how I got there. I remembered nothing after pulling onto the highway from the hospital parking lot. My thoughts were consumed by Jenny and the tasks ahead.

4

"It's for you." My wife Karen handed me the phone as I walked into the kitchen from the carport.

I kissed her before taking the receiver from her hand. "Hello," I answered.

"Is this Blake Thomas?" asked the voice on the other end of the telephone.

"Yes it is."

"Blake," the voice continued, "my name is Walter Grant. I understand you were with Jenny Curtis last night."

"Yes I was. Are you a family member?" I questioned.

"No, I'm from the church Jenny attended. I'm sorry to bother you at home, but I just missed you at the hospital. The nurse I spoke with said you were planning on helping with Jenny's funeral arrangements. Is that right?" he asked.

"Well, I was hoping.... Yes, I was intending to help organize some sort of service." I was shocked by my response. I had just waived an opportunity to free myself

23

from the whole situation.

"Perhaps we could meet today and discuss the plans," Mr. Grant suggested.

"Today would be just fine. Say around ten o'clock?" I proposed.

By this time Karen had picked up on the conversation and began shaking her head. "What about the Easter egg hunt?" she whispered.

I nodded, suggesting that I had everything under control.

"Great, I'll see you at Jenny's place then. Do you need directions?" Mr. Grant asked.

"Yes, please," I responded as I motioned for Karen to hand me a pencil and some paper. I wrote down the address. "Good-bye and thank you," I said and hung up the phone.

"Blake, what about the Easter egg hunt? You promised the kids and what are you doing anyway?" Karen asked as she snuggled in for a welcome home hug and another kiss.

Karen and I would have been perfect subjects for a study of opposites attracting. But our differences only strengthened our relationship. We had learned, over the previous eight years of marriage, how to compensate for each other's weaknesses: I did things the way I always had and Karen patiently patched things up. She never got angry, unless someone threatened our children, so I knew I was nearing the danger zone.

"I figured we'd do that this afternoon," I replied, hoping she would assume that was my intent all along.

"And what's this service you're meeting about at ten?"

"Nothing, just a funeral," I casually answered.

"How, may I ask, did you get into the funeral business?" she questioned.

"You know, I'm not sure. It just kind of happened."

"What, did you answer a newspaper ad--Blake what's going on?" she asked even more confused.

"I'm sorry Karen. Last night, I took care of a lady, one of my old teachers and she died. She doesn't have any family, so I'm helping someone from her church arrange a funeral." I continued. "I figure I can catch a couple hours of sleep right now and then meet with this Mr. Grant for an hour. That will still leave plenty of time to decorate and hide eggs."

I could tell Karen was not convinced I would have time to accomplish everything, but I continued expressing confidence in my own organizational abilities.

"And if Mr. Grant needs you for more than an hour, then what?" she asked.

"Then I'll finish with him tomorrow after church. Now

I'm going to lie down. Can you wake me in two hours please?" I requested.

Karen nodded and smiled. "I love you," she said as she walked with me to the bedroom, "and someday I'll understand why."

Her warm humor comforted me as I slipped into my pajamas and crawled under the covers.

I usually had no difficulty falling asleep after a night shift, but my mind was racing with thoughts of Jenny.

"Red shoes? What did you do, steal them from your sister?" the kids teased.

I was proud of the gym shoes my parents had just bought me. It had not bothered me that they came from a department store instead of the mall, and I had even ignored the fact that they were out of my size in blue. I had looked forward to walking down the halls at school with shoes like everyone else's. Now I felt like crying, but I resisted the urge. My brothers had taught me that "tough guys don't cry," especially at school. So I ran. I ran to get away from the cruelty of my own peers and ended up in the only place I felt safe.

"Hi Blake, what brings you here? Class doesn't start for another half hour."

"Hi Mrs. Curtis. I know, I just... " I hesitated. "I just

wanted to come in and practice my typing."

Mrs. Curtis smiled. "That's very commendable. Is there anything I can help you with, as far as practicing I mean?"

I just stood staring at the ground. Unfortunately, my feet were on the ground, and the red shoes were on my feet. I could not restrain myself any longer. "Why does everybody hate me?" I sobbed.

Mrs. Curtis took me in her arms and whispered softly in my ear. "Everyone doesn't hate you Blake, they just don't understand people like us. You and I don't care about the same things they do."

"What do you mean?" I asked between tears.

"Blake, you need to rise above them. Be the kind of person you'd want for a friend, otherwise you'll be just like them."

"Blake, it's quarter to ten," Karen called from the other room.

"I'm awake," I said as I dragged myself out of the bed and got dressed.

As I walked into the kitchen, Karen handed me a glass of orange juice. I stood silently, staring out the window.

"You didn't sleep did you?" Karen asked.

I shook my head and turned, but before I could speak,

I was attacked from behind.

"Daddy!" Kelsi screamed with laughter as she wrapped her arms around my leg and sat on my foot. Teryl quickly followed suit and planted himself on my other foot.

This was a Saturday morning ritual in our home. I set my juice on the counter and walked around the room lifting my children with each step. "Mom, someone's attacking me, help!" I protested.

Though fatigued, my children seemed to energize me with their tireless enthusiasm for life. I often thought the world would do better if everyone viewed things from a child's perspective.

I fell to the floor and began tickling the children as usual. Six-year-old Kelsi's laugh always turned to a high-pitched squeal, capable of warding off even the boldest attacker. The deep, adult-like chuckle of three-year-old Teryl never failed to delight me to the point of almost uncontrollable laughter.

I gained my composure and stood up. "I have to go," I said.

"What about the Easter egg hunt, Daddy?" Kelsi asked.

Teryl just nodded in agreement, accepting Kelsi as suitable voice for both of them.

THE SHIFT

"I'll only be a little while. You help Mom get things ready and we'll color the eggs when I get back," I responded.

"Is that your little while, or a kid's little while?" Kelsi asked.

"It's about an hour, now help your mother," I said, trying not to laugh.

Sensing that there was more to the previous night than I had told her, Karen followed me out to the carport.

"What really happened last night?" she asked.

"She said something to me just before she died. I don't know what she meant, but I can't get it off my mind." I continued. "I almost feel like she was warning me or giving me some advice or something."

Karen smiled her understanding smile and kissed me on the cheek. "You'd better go before you're late. We'll talk about it when you get back."

5

It was only a short drive to the address Mr. Grant had given me. At the base of the foothills, on the east edge of town, I turned down a long, tree-lined driveway. The sun broke through the leaves, sending spears of light to pierce the green canopy. At the end of the drive stood a small but beautiful old home. Dormer windows, transoms and a covered porch added charm to the brick structure. I estimated it to be between eighty and ninety years old. Sadly, the landscaping appeared to be nearly as aged. Untrimmed rose bushes surrounded the front entry, and the grass stood over a foot tall. The occasional tulip could be seen making its way through the overgrown flower garden by the steps.

There was a car parked in front of the house. Standing near the front porch was a tall, stately gentleman with greying hair and a mustache to match. He approached as I got out of my car.

"Blake?" he asked, extending his hand.

Nodding, I responded to his gesture. "You must be Mr.

Grant," I said. "I'm pleased to meet you."

"I appreciate you coming here this morning," he said. I realize you must be tired after working all night. Hopefully this won't take long." His gentle manner quickly dispelled any reluctance I had about meeting with him. He continued. "You're probably wondering why I requested your help."

"Actually, I am a bit curious," I said.

"Jenny was pretty well confined to her home during the past several years, so she didn't know many people. I realize there will be people from the church at her funeral, but none of them really knew her. I just thought it would be nice if there were a few of her friends in attendance."

"Glad I can help," I said. "Is that all you would like me to do, attend the funeral?"

"I was hoping you would also give a tribute to Jenny," he said hesitantly.

I felt like an anvil had just been dropped on my chest. There was nothing I hated more than speaking in public. To make matters worse, I was not that acquainted with Jenny. How could I pay tribute to someone I had not seen in fifteen years?

"I'm not sure I could do that," I stammered. "I didn't know her that well."

THE SHIFT

"How long have you known Jenny?" he asked.

"Since Junior High School," was my reply. "She was my type teacher, but that was a long time ago. Last night was the first time I'd seen her in years."

"I see," he said. "Still, you offered to help with the arrangements. Why?"

"I kind of felt I owed it to her," I said as I began staring down the driveway. My voice slowed as I continued. "She did a lot for me back then."

"Give it back!" I screamed at the boy who had just taken my type eraser.

As I approached him, he threw it over my head to another boy who had come up behind me. I turned to see the second boy throwing my eraser, like a basketball, into the waste basket. I walked to the basket and looked inside. There, next to some chewed bubble gum and a few pieces of scrunched-up paper was my type eraser. I reached inside to retrieve it.

As my hand entered the waste basket, the whole class chimed in unison, "scrounge!"

Embarrassed, I returned to my seat. My face was red and hot. I picked up my books and headed for the door.

Unaware that she was in the room, I gasped when Mrs. Curtis stepped in front of me, preventing my retreat. "Take your seat, Blake," she said sternly and walked to the front of the classroom.

Without saying a word, Mrs. Curtis picked up the waste basket and placed it on the table. With the entire class watching, she took a type eraser from the boy who had stolen mine and dropped it into the garbage.

"Do you want it back?" Mrs Curtis asked the boy.

"No, I'll just get another one," he said.

"Why won't you get this one?" she questioned.

"Because it ain't worth it," he said.

Mrs. Curtis walked over to her desk, opened a drawer and pulled out her purse. From her purse she took a twenty dollar bill. Returning to the table, she dropped the money next to the boy's eraser.

"Now is it worth it?" she asked.

"You bet," the boy returned.

Pointing to the waste basket, she challenged him. "Then come scrounge it out."

The boy started to get up, but sat down again when others in the class began snickering.

"Blake," Mrs. Curtis asked, "would you like this?"

I nodded.

She motioned for me to join her at the front. I stood next to her and she pointed at the waste basket. I reached in and recovered the money.

THE SHIFT

"Isn't it a shame that someone would surrender something of value because of a little name calling?" she asked. "Is Blake the only one here smart enough to understand that?"

She took the eraser from the garbage and returned it to the owner.

"Blake?" Mr. Grant placed his hand on my shoulder.

"I'm sorry," I said, startled by his touch and oblivious to his last comment. "What was it you said?"

"I said it sounds to me like you could deliver a fine tribute. Part of the reason I wanted to meet here was so you could learn a little more about Jenny. You can see if there is anything inside that might help. What do you say?"

His persuasive argument left me with little choice. "I'll do it," I said.

"Excellent. Now shall we go inside?" he asked rhetorically.

I followed him onto the front porch. He slid his hand along the top of the door frame and produced a key that opened the large wooden door.

In my experience, homes belonging to the senior population were usually decorated in one of two ways. They were either packed so full of furniture and accessories that there was little unoccupied space, or so elegantly furnished that you wondered if anyone actually lived there. Jenny's was neither.

Inside was a scantily furnished living room and connected dining area. Two open doors revealed a small kitchen and bedroom. I could see the bathroom on the other side of the kitchen. There was a closed door which presumably led to the attic. Large windows allowed the sunshine to filter through the house. The hardwood floor squeaked under the floral rug as we made our way across the room.

"I'll show you around," Mr. Grant offered.

"That would be great," I said as we started for the first open door.

A refrigerator, a gas range, a washing machine and an electric dryer lined the outside kitchen wall like a row of disciplined soldiers. The cupboards, along with the rest of the house, were painted white. Worn linoleum exposed a bare wood floor in front of the sink. There was nothing on the counter top--not even the requisite bowl of plastic fruit.

We proceeded to the bathroom. It was barely large enough for the fixtures it contained. A small vanity was tucked behind the door and rested next to the toilet, which sat directly in front of the oversized claw-foot bathtub.

THE SHIFT

The bath mat spanned the entire distance from the tub to the base of the toilet. Above the toilet hung a picture of a lighthouse. A small medicine cabinet and mirror were mounted over the sink.

Walking back through the kitchen and dining area, we entered the bedroom. The bed nearly filled the entire room, its sides reaching from the wall to the door. A tall, freestanding wardrobe towered behind the door, which supported a full length mirror. At the foot of the bed was a dressing table adorned with crocheted doilies. There was barely sufficient room to open the drawers without hitting the bed. The remaining corner was occupied by a wooden rocking chair. Atop the bed was a hand stitched quilt.

Returning to the dining area, I noted a small wooden table with two chairs. On the table was a telephone.

We moved into the living room where our tour had begun. A brick fireplace made up the back wall. There was a long sofa against the wall to the right. On the left, next to the front door were a nearly empty bookshelf and a coat tree. An upholstered platform rocker sat in the center of the room, in front of the bookshelf. Next to the chair was an oddly positioned side table with a large black Bible resting on top. The table prevented passage to the far end of the room. On the wall directly in front of the chair, above the sofa, was a picture of Jesus.

Amazed by my surroundings, I had remained silent during the tour. It was not the simplicity of the furnishings nor the unusual arrangement that caught my attention, but the fact that nothing matched. There did not appear to be a "set" of anything. Even the chairs at the dining room table were from different origins.

Mr. Grant broke the now uncomfortable silence. "Well, what do you think?"

"It's not what I expected," I said. "So what's upstairs?"

"A whole lot of empty," was his reply.

"You mean nothing? No books, no magazines?" I asked.

"I mean nothing. You can look if you'd like," he said, pointing to the attic door.

"No, I believe you," I said. "I'm just surprised, that's all."

"Well, you don't need to be. It hasn't always been this way."

"What do you mean?" I asked.

"It used to be furnished like any other house. Then Jenny's husband died and her health began to fail. She decided there was more here than one person could use. She had no family, so she started giving things away to anyone who needed them."

"How did she know who needed them?" I asked.

THE SHIFT

"That's where I came in," he said. "Jenny would decide to give something away and then contact me to see if someone at church could use it. I'd find a worthy recipient and they'd receive the item without knowing the source of their good fortune. That's the way   Jenny   wanted it."

"So this was all she had left?" I questioned.

"Not exactly. The furniture was hers, but she sold the house to a developer several years ago. Part of the agreement was that she could remain here for the rest of her life. She was able to live on the money from the sale. With her death, the remainder will be given to charity."

"I've never heard of anyone giving so much to strangers," I commented.

Mr. Grant glanced at the picture above the sofa and smiled. "You haven't, huh?" he asked, chuckling quietly to himself. "Feel free to look around. Maybe you can find something that will help with your tribute."

"Thanks," I said. "So how much time should this tribute take?"

"I'll leave that to you," he said. We're just planning a small service at the grave-side. I don't expect more than ten or fifteen people."

I began exploring the rooms, but found few items that could help me define Jenny. Besides the basics needed to run a household, all I discovered was clothing and one file box. Inside the box were some old receipts and a few legal documents detailing the sale of her house. To my surprise, I did not even find a typewriter. I walked back to the living room, contemplating the events of the morning.

"Did you find anything?" Mr. Grant asked. He was sitting, thumbing through the Bible.

"A little," was my reply.

"I believe I'll take this and use it in my remarks Monday," he said handing me the Bible.

It was large and heavy. The black leather binding was worn from frequent use. Each yellowing page was smudged near the edge. I noted several passages underlined in red. A black and white photograph of Jenny and her husband was glued inside the front cover. "They made a handsome couple," I said.

"Yes they did," he agreed and reached for the book.

Extending my hand to return the bible, I caught sight of my watch. It was half past eleven. "The kids," I said aloud. "I've got to get home."

6

Karen worked by the rule of doubles when it came to my time keeping. If I told her I would be gone a certain length of time, she would double it and expect me at the newly calculated hour. It was no surprise then, to see the children at the kitchen table coloring Easter eggs when I arrived home.

"Hi Daddy," Kelsi called. "We started without you."

"I'm glad you did, honey. Where's Mom?" I asked.

"She's hiding eggs of course," she replied as though offended by a question with such an obvious answer.

Kelsi's apron was clean and her eggs were smartly decorated with stripes and stars and other indescribable markings. Teryl, on the other hand, had removed his apron. His shirt, face, hands and eggs were a soft shade of purple-grey-green. Colored water was everywhere.

"Is that the last of your eggs?" I asked.

"Yup," was Kelsi's reply.

Though old enough to speak, Teryl was a man of few words. His older sister did all the talking for him, so a handful of simple gestures and an occasional grunt got him whatever he needed. He smiled and handed me his eggs.

Karen came in as we were cleaning up the mess. "I see you made it," she said sarcastically.

"I was going to call, but the only phone at Mrs. Curtis' was one of those old things with a dial. I wasn't sure if I remembered how to use it," I quipped in response.

"So did you finish?" she asked as she gathered the soggy newspaper from the table.

"I don't need to go back to her house if that's what you mean. But, I won't be finished until after the service. Mr. Grant asked me to give a tribute."

"And you actually agreed to do it? Blake, are you feeling okay?" she asked.

"No," I said laughing, "I'm tired and vulnerable, so don't ask me to do anything." I carried Teryl to the sink and washed his multicolored hands and face.

"I promise, after the Easter egg hunt, you can take a nap," she said.

Karen took the remaining eggs outside and hid them while I put Teryl in a clean shirt. Easter baskets in hand, the two children and I headed to the back yard for the big hunt.

Behind our house was a large lawn with several fruit

trees on either side. A tall hedge separated our property from that of our neighbors. Near the back property line were a sandbox and swing set for the children. The center space remained open, making it available for a variety of activities. It was this area we called the meadow because of the wild-flowers that blossomed each year. Mowing the yard was avoided each spring until all the blooms were gone. The tall grass and carpet of flowers provided a perfect setting for our Easter egg hunt.

The children were allowed to find only the eggs they had colored, and three plastic eggs filled with a candy surprise. Kelsi was off to the meadow as soon as we left the house, her contagious giggle echoing as she bounded through the grass. By the time Teryl and I arrived, she already had two eggs safely in her basket. Karen took Teryl by the hand and they set out to seek the hidden treasures. It was amusing to watch Teryl navigate through grass equal in length to his legs. He burst into joyous laughter when he discovered his first egg. Soon, the successful hunters joined me under the apple tree. Karen went into the house and returned with a large blanket and a picnic lunch.

"Daddy, why do we have Easter eggs?" Kelsi asked as she removed the blue shell from one of her boiled eggs.

"Well," I hesitated as I formulated an answer suitable

for a six-year-old, "they help us remember what Jesus did for us."

"How?" she asked as she stuffed the entire egg into her mouth.

"When a baby chicken is born, it starts inside an egg. Its body grows inside the egg until it's strong enough to break the shell and come out. When it does finally come out, a new life enters the world." Carefully selecting my words, I continued. "When Jesus died, his body was put inside a tomb. When he was ready, his body became alive again. Like the chicken coming out of the egg, he came out of the tomb with a new life."

"Is that what 'resected' means?" she questioned between bites of a bologna sandwich.

"Yes, that's what *resurrected* means," I said holding back a laugh. "And because Jesus was resurrected, we can all be resurrected after we die."

"Even Mrs. Curtis?" she asked.

Her question stunned me. I did not think Kelsi was aware of what had been going on in my life. Karen and I looked at each other. She just shook her head and shrugged her shoulders.

"Yes, Kelsi, even Mrs. Curtis," I responded.

After lunch, we sent the children to play and I retired to the bedroom to prepare for some well-deserved sleep.

THE SHIFT

Karen came into the room as I was slipping under the covers.

"What did Mrs. Curtis say last night?" she asked.

"She said, 'remember the shift key'. Weird, huh?"

Looking at me with her insightful smile, Karen ran her fingers through my hair. "Why is that so hard to figure out?" she asked. "You know what a shift key does. Just go from there."

That was too simple. Surely there was more to it than that. I tried to come up with a good argument to Karen's line of thinking, but it was of no use. I was too tired. "You may be right," I said, "maybe it is that simple. Thank You."

"You're welcome, now get some sleep," she said.

7

I was awakened by the sound of voices. I looked
at the clock and saw that it was just after nine thirty.
Knowing Karen would have put the children to bed at
eight, I wondered who she was talking to. Climbing out
of bed, I changed from my pajamas to a pair of jeans and
a T-shirt. My bare feet were cold as I hurried toward the
source of the voices.

"If I'd known you were awake, I would have called
you," Karen said. She was standing by the front door
talking to Mr. Grant, who was just about to leave.

"I guess you two have met" I said, looking at Mr.
Grant.

"Yes, we have," he replied. "I was just giving your
wife the details of the service, but now I can tell you."

I pointed to the sofa. "Then why don't you come back
in and sit down for a minute?" I offered.

Mr. Grant took a seat, then Karen handed him a large
book she was holding. He laid the book on the table in
front of the sofa. "I also brought this for you," he said

pointing at the book.

I looked at the hard-bound book laying in front of us. There were no markings on the dark green cover. It did not close tightly, but fanned open from the broad spine to the front edge of the pages. Corners of paper could be seen emerging from its three open sides. I reached down and lifted the front cover to reveal its contents. Inside, some of the pages were covered with newspaper clippings, photographs, letters and other assorted items. Each facing page had a handwritten date and an entry made below it.

"Where did it come from?" I asked.

"Jenny," Mr. Grant responded. "After you left this morning, I went back to secure the house. When checking to see that the windows in the living room were locked, I bumped into the table next to the rocking chair. I dislodged a drawer in the table and found this in the drawer."

"Do you know what it is? I mean, did you know about it before?" I asked.

"No," he replied, "that was the first time I'd seen it. I haven't taken the time to go through it. I thought you could do that."

It seemed strange that Mr. Grant had made this discovery, but left it for me to explore. Perhaps he felt the same reluctance I did about it. Unlike the Bible, or even her house, this was personal. It did not seem right to probe into Jenny's personal life without her permission.

"Yeah, maybe I'll go through it later," I said, closing the book. "Now, tell me about her service."

"Right, she will be buried in Oakville Cemetery, next to her husband," he said. "You need to be there a little before ten. I'll welcome everyone, we'll sing a hymn, have a prayer and then I'll give my remarks. Your tribute will be next, then we will conclude with a prayer of dedication on the grave. Do you have any questions?" he asked.

"No, that sounds great," I responded.

"Well, I'd better be on my way." He stood up. "It was a pleasure to meet you, Karen."

"Nice meeting you too," Karen returned.

We accompanied him to the door and stood outside until he had driven away.

"What are you going to do with that journal?" Karen asked.

"Nothing right now." I took her by the hand and led her to the bedroom.

We sat together on the bed to watch the television news. Karen fell asleep before it had ended, so I turned off the television and put a blanket over her. Returning to the front room, I opened the journal.

I decided it would be all right to look at the photos and papers as long as I did not read any of Jenny's written entries. Somewhere near the middle of the book, there was a clipping from the Oakville Junior High newspaper. It was an article about the student elections. I did not know any of the students listed in the article, but I knew about the election process.

"People don't even like talking to me. Why would they want to vote for me?" I asked as Mrs. Curtis turned and faced me.

"Blake, the student body needs good leaders. You are a good leader. This might be hard for you to believe, but being a leader is more than having people who will follow you. A good leader sets a proper example and tries to do the right thing, not just the popular thing. I am describing you, Blake. Won't you at least consider running for the student council?"

"But I'll lose," I protested.

"If you run, you will be a winner regardless of how the election turns out. If you choose not to run, you will be admitting defeat without even trying."

Knowing any rebuttal was now useless, I gave in to her pleading. "All right, I'll run. But only if you'll help me," I added.

THE SHIFT

"I've already started helping you. I submitted your name for the election yesterday and signed up as the faculty advisor this morning," was her smug reply.

Closing the book, I went back to the bedroom and Karen's side.

8

Easter Morning was a delight in our home. Our children were aware of the worldly aspects of the holiday, but Karen and I did our best to relate these distractions to the true meaning. For me, this Easter had taken on a bitter-sweet ambiance, but it was Easter just the same. Karen always got up early to assure that the rest of us awoke to the smell of fresh baked cinnamon rolls. We enjoyed breakfast together as a family. Before getting ready for church, we read the story of the first Easter from the Bible.

As I was getting dressed, my mind wrestled with two separate, yet related questions: What was Jenny trying to tell me and what was I going to tell others in tribute to her?

Karen interrupted my thoughts. "I think we're ready," she said, poking her head past the partially open bedroom door.

"Let's go then," I said.

Outside, the crisp morning air filled our lungs with

springtime. The sun peaked over the hills, creating an array of color on the dew that still bathed the grass. Though we made the trip weekly, the beauty of the day made our twenty minutes journey to Garden City, a pleasure. The children played quietly in the back seat. Karen and I held hands, but neither of us spoke. Once at church, we seated ourselves near the front of the chapel. We found that this provided fewer distractions for the children and more incentive for me to stay awake during the meeting.

I felt warm inside as I listened to the Easter messages.

"Jesus gave us a most valuable gift on the third day," the speaker said from the pulpit. "But we must not forget the gift he gave prior to his death and resurrection. He lived a life dedicated to blessing others, lifting them to new heights. Sometimes this was accomplished through miracles, but usually it came by way of his teachings and by his example. He inspired people to believe in themselves, to work harder, to reach higher..."

Those words struck a familiar chord.

"I told you I'd lose," I said, staring at the election results posted outside the Principal's office.

"And I said you'd be a winner just for trying," Mrs. Curtis returned.

THE SHIFT

"I didn't know what you meant then and I still don't," I replied.

"You told me you had no chance of winning, but look at the results. You were only a few votes behind your opponent. Think about what that means; there are 137 students who felt you could do the job. You need to start seeing the same Blake they see."

"But I still lost," I said, shaking my head.

"There's where you are wrong. You just won the support of 137 peers. This is your chance to shine, Blake. If you work a little harder and reach a little higher, you can accomplish anything you want."

"Not this year," I said.

"Remember I told you I signed up to be faculty advisor to the student council?" she asked.

The twinkle in her eye told me she was up to something. "Yes," I answered dubiously.

"Well, there are two non-elected positions on the student council." Mrs. Curtis smiled with satisfaction as she continued. "As faculty advisor, it is my responsibility to appoint a representative from each grade. The council meets in the faculty lounge at three. I'll expect you there on time."

I could feel the excitement building inside. I just had

to say something. "I think I get it," I whispered to Karen.

"Shhhh," she said, pressing her finger to her lips.

"But I..."

Karen cut me off. "It can wait until after church," she whispered.

Restlessly, I waited for the meeting to end. Immediately following the last "amen," I took Karen's hands in mine, looked her in the eye and exclaimed, "I know what Mrs. Curtis meant! The shift key, it raises the other keys on the typewriter to a higher level. It takes an ordinary letter of the alphabet and lifts it, making it capable of leading a sentence or a proper noun." My voice was increasing in volume.

"People are beginning to stare," Karen said calmly. She turned and smiled at the few people still occupying the surrounding pews.

I lowered my voice and continued. "That's what she did for me. She took an ordinary student and helped raise him to the level of a leader."

"That makes sense," she said. "Mrs. Curtis must have been a wise woman." She stood up and took Kelsi by the hand. "Let's go home."

Teryl had fallen asleep, so I laid his head on my shoulder and followed the others to the car. I was looking forward to a quiet afternoon with my children and the

THE SHIFT

other wise woman in my life.

"Dad," Kelsi asked as we started for home, "how could Jesus still be alive after the wicked men killed him?"

Our drive home was often spent answering the children's questions or discussing things learned at church. It was a good way to remember the messages of the day and frequently provided invaluable teaching opportunities.

I thought for a minute before answering. "All of us have a spirit that lives inside our body," I started. "When we die, our spirit and body separate. When Jesus was on the cross, his body was the only thing that died. It was put in the tomb, but his spirit went to heaven." I watched Kelsi's face through the rear-view mirror as I spoke. She seemed to understand, so I continued. "After three days, Jesus' spirit went back into his body and he became resurrected."

"Can he die again?" Kelsi asked.

"No," I said, "once a person is resurrected, they can never die again."

"When will your friend, Mrs. Curtis be resurrected?"

"Not until Jesus comes again," I replied. "Many people who died before Jesus were resurrected when he was. Everyone else will have to wait until he comes to earth again.

"But her spirit is still alive, right?" she asked.
"Right, it's just in another place for now," I answered.

<u>9</u>

Knowing that Sunday night was usually slow in the emergency center, I took Jenny's journal to work with me. There were no patients waiting when I arrived. Pat was sitting at the nurse's station reading a book.

"You cleared the place out for me, thank you," I said.

"It's my Easter present to you. I'm glad you like it," she returned.

"You probably didn't see many people with it being a holiday," I stated.

"No, we didn't. In fact, I can't remember when it has been this slow," she said. "There hasn't been anyone in here for over three hours, so I wouldn't be surprised if you went all night without seeing a patient."

A statement like that would normally discourage me, but that night, nothing could have made me more happy. "Sounds good to me," I said.

Pat got her things from the lounge and walked toward the hallway leading to the time clock. "How are your funeral plans coming?" she asked.

"They're coming along well, thank you," I said.

She nodded and continued on her way.

Gathering my things, I made my way to the nurse's lounge. Michelle was just settling in at her desk, so I went back to speak to her.

"Do you have a lot of homework tonight?" I asked.

"Yes, I have a test on the cardiac system tomorrow," she replied.

"Pat said it has been quiet, so you may have the whole night to study," I said.

"That would be great," she responded. "So how did it go with Mrs. Curtis?"

"I think it went fine. Of course I haven't done much. A man from her church has made most of the arrangements," I said.

"Then you got off pretty easy?" she asked.

"No, I'm giving a tribute at her service tomorrow," I replied.

"Sounds like you could use some study time too. I'll try to leave you alone," she promised.

The sound of rubbing nylons interrupted our conversation and signaled Martha's approach.

"Did you get your homework done?" Martha asked.

"I beg your pardon," I said, confused by her question.

"Didn't your type teacher give you an assignment?"

THE SHIFT

she questioned as she sat in a nearby chair.

"Oh, that," I laughed. "As a matter of fact, I did complete the assignment."

"I know it's none of my business," she said, "but sometime I would be interested in knowing what you decided she meant."

My continued contemplation of Jenny's dying words made me realized how narrow my initial understanding had been. Added to the events of the past few days, those words had changed my perspective of life.

"Basically, she was telling me to follow a good example and help others," I volunteered.

Martha looked baffled. "May I ask how you came to that conclusion?"

"Jenny Curtis was more than my type teacher. Though I didn't realize it at the time, she was teaching me to believe in myself and to reach higher. Since her death, I've discovered that her whole life was dedicated to reaching out and lifting those in need."

"So where does the shift key fit in?" she asked.

"The shift key lifts its neighbors, doesn't it? I asked rhetorically.

Martha nodded in understanding. "It sounds like you had a profitable weekend." She stood up to leave. "I'm glad things turned out so well."

"I'll be in the back if you need me," I said to Michelle. I returned to the lounge and sat in the chair.

The journal was quite heavy and difficult to balance because of its wedge shape. I laid it on my lap and began flipping through the pages. Still feeling it was not my place to read the journal entries, I looked only at the many photographs and newspaper clippings. Most of them had to do with the school or Jenny's students. As I worked my way through the book, I began to see a pattern. Everything seemed to relate to a select group of people. Jenny had chosen one or two struggling students each year and helped them reach their potential. The articles and pictures recorded their progress and accomplishments. I assumed that the written entries on the facing pages had to do with the related clipping or photo. It was no surprise to find a picture of the student council the year I had been an appointed representative. In it, I was smiling from ear-to-ear and Jenny stood next to me, displaying a similar expression.

Near the back of the book, the newspaper clippings began to change, obviously near the time of Jenny's retirement. The emphasis shifted to the achievements of her students as adults. One particular newspaper clipping stuck out. The rest of the journal had the handwritten entries on the left hand page with the photos and clippings on the facing page. This one was reversed. It was attached to the left page and the handwritten entry was on the right. I lifted the page containing the writing and discovered several subsequent pages, both left and right, containing nothing but writing. I returned to the clipping. It was Jenny's husband's obituary. Beneath it Jenny had written, "Out of the mouth of babes." Curious as to what this meant, but referring to my previous sentiment, I did not feel I could read the entry pertaining to the obituary.

I laid the journal aside and began reflecting on my experience at church. As I thought about Jenny's words, I remembered her desire was to help others. Now that she was gone, her journal was the only source of her wisdom. I picked it up and began to read.

Jenny wrote about the love she had for her husband and the pain she felt at his passing. She expressed guilt about the conditions surrounding his death. Each morning for several weeks, she had been helping some neighbors, the parents of new twins, by taking their six-year-old daughter to school. One morning, Jenny's husband was not feeling well and she wanted to stay home with him. He insisted she take the girl to school and that he would be fine. Jenny returned to find her husband dead in their bed. She recorded her feelings as she prayed for solace, asking to know that Pete, her husband, had died peacefully and not in pain. Relief came the evening of the funeral when Lea, the little girl Jenny had been taking to school, came to visit. Jenny's journal entry read:

Lea came to visit me this evening. When she came in, she asked if she could see Pete again. I explained to her that he was gone and would not be back. I told Lea that the funeral was a way of saying good-bye to Pete. She told me she had seen him that afternoon at the grave-side. She said he was standing next to me. I asked her what Pete was doing and she said, "Nothing, he was just smiling." I held Lea in my arms and wept tears of joy. There is peace in my heart once more. I thank God for this little girl. "Out of the mouth of babes"

<u>10</u>

I altered my usual route home so I could drive by
Jenny's house. As I sat in the driveway staring at the
unoccupied home, I wondered how things might have
been different had I kept in contact with Jenny after Junior
High School. Knowing this question would remain
forever unanswered, I wished for only one thing. In my
heart, I needed to know if I had correctly interpreted
Jenny's final expression. "If I could just speak to you one
last time," I said aloud.

Jenny's journal was beside me on the car seat. It had
fallen open as I drove. I reached down to close it and
caught my hand on the flap of an envelope attached to the
open page. I removed the contents of the envelope. It was
an invitation to an Oakville Junior High Awards Banquet.

"It's an invitation to the awards banquet," Mrs. Curtis
said.

"Why do I need an invitation?" I asked. "You said the
Student Council was supposed to attend."

"That's right, but we sent invitations to everyone who would be receiving awards tonight. This one is yours.

"We reviewed the list of award recipients in council meeting yesterday. My name wasn't on the list," I insisted.

"It wasn't on the list because I didn't want you, or the other council members to know," she said.

"Is this a real award, or is this something you've arranged just for me?" I asked fearfully.

"I wasn't going to tell you." She continued. "You have changed so much since I first met you. You have become a respected leader among your peers. I'm proud of you, Blake. No, this award isn't from me, it's the leadership award. As you know, the recipient is determined by the vote of the entire student body. You earned this award."

"Thank you," I said, "I'll never forget what you've done for me."

I turned my car around and drove home. By the time I arrived, Karen had the children dressed and ready for Jenny's service. Time seemed to be advancing at half speed as I showered and put on my favorite suit. Sensing my need for a state of solitude, Karen kept the children occupied and avoided engaging me in any real conversation. When I finished getting dressed, I said a prayer to receive guidance for the day, especially the next few hours. Karen and I put the children in the car and we drove to the cemetery.

We found Mr. Grant by the open grave. The mortician had just arrived and was standing by the back of the open hearse. For the first time since Friday night, I was unable to control my emotions and tears began to form in my eyes. Karen and the children watched as Mr. Grant and I helped the mortician and the sexton. We lifted the casket from the hearse and placed it on boards over the open ground. I went back and stood by Karen who took my hand and squeezed it tightly. Wrapped in my recent flood of emotion, I was completely unaware of what was happening around me.

"Ladies and gentlemen," Mr. Grant started, "I would like to welcome everyone here as we honor the life of Jenny Curtis. I know she would be pleased by the outpouring of love that is here this morning. Each of you is here because Jenny somehow touched your life. I know there are many others Jenny touched anonymously, and I'm sure they are with us in their hearts..."

Mr. Grant concluded his welcome and announced the program.

The gathered crowd began to sing the hymn. Though the harmonization was typical of such a group, the volume was that of a much larger assembly. I lifted my head and looked around. To my amazement, I was surrounded by well over a hundred people. Tears began to flow again as I realized the magnitude of Jenny's influence.

After the prayer, Mr. Grant read some passages from Jenny's Bible, then proceeded with his eulogy. "I think it most appropriate that Jenny's passing should occur on the very weekend set aside to remember the death and resurrection of the Savior Jesus Christ. Like him, Jenny Curtis spent her life teaching and doing good for others. Both left behind a legacy of service and an example of love we should all try to emulate. Let me close by reading a verse Jenny had underlined in her Bible. The 113th Psalm, verse seven reads, 'He raiseth up the poor out of the dust, and lifteth the needy out of the dunghill.' I believe this was her inspiration, may she be ours."

Mr. Grant concluded and introduced me as the next speaker. I stepped forward and stood next to him in front of Jenny's casket. As I scanned the crowd, I saw many familiar faces: Some belonged to friends from school, others I recognized from photographs in Jenny's journal.

"I had the honor of being with Mrs. Curtis when she died," I began. "The last words she spoke to me, like the first so many years ago, will have a lasting impact on my life and hopefully on the lives of others. As her student, I learned to type; as my teacher, she taught me to live. She encouraged me to improve my life by serving other people and by serving God. Jesus taught that when we serve our brothers and sisters, we serve him. As God's children, we are all brothers and sisters. I believe Mrs. Curtis is here with us today, and I know that through each of us, her legacy can endure." With tear filled eyes, I continued. "Jenny Curtis will live on only if we look around and help those in need, if we offer a kind word and give some encouragement to the discouraged. We must not kick those who are already down, but offer them our hand and help them up. Our abundance should be shared with those who may otherwise go without. In short, we must love our neighbor."

Thoughts continued to come into my mind, but I concluded. Perhaps the remaining thoughts were only for me. I returned to my family and listened to the words of dedication. Sniffing could be heard all around, but I was confident it was due to tears of joy. I felt Jenny's presence just as I had in the emergency room after she died.

As the service concluded and the crowd began to disperse, Mr. Grant came over and handed me Jenny's Bible. "She would have wanted you to have this," he said.

I took the Bible and without saying a word, we shook

hands and expressed our appreciation for each other. Silently, I thanked Jenny for allowing us to meet.

Silence continued its reign as we left the cemetery. At that moment, I resolved in my heart to change my life. I believe it no accident that Jenny's death coincided with Easter. For me, that shift was the beginning of a new life.

At home, I sat in the front room reflecting on the events of the past few days. Karen was in the kitchen with the children. Teryl was playing with some toys on the floor and Kelsi was looking through Jenny's Bible.

"Daddy, who is this lady?" Kelsi asked as she came into the room with the Bible in her hand. She had it open to the front cover and was looking at the picture of Jenny and her husband.

"That's Mrs. Curtis," I answered.

"I thought so," she said, "but she looks younger here."

"What do you mean she looks younger?" I questioned. "You've never met her."

"No, but I've seen her," she responded.

A chill went down my spine. "When did you see her?" I asked, motioning for her to join me on the sofa.

Karen had overheard the conversation and was standing in the doorway.

"Today, she was standing by you when you were talking," was Kelsi's matter-of-fact reply.

THE SHIFT

Unable to speak, I swept her into my arms and began to weep.

Karen knelt in front of us. Putting one hand on my leg and the other on Kelsi's back, she asked, "Kelsi, what was Mrs. Curtis doing?"

"Nothing mommy," she answered, "just smiling."

Karen nodded.

"Mommy?" Kelsi asked, "why is daddy crying?"

"Because you've made him very happy." Karen took Kelsi from my arms and sent her to play with Teryl. She sat next to me and put her arm around my shoulder. "Out of the mouth of babes," she said.

Epilogue

I met Mr. Grant at the cemetery the next week to watch as Jenny's headstone was lifted into place. With anticipation we observed the workman set the granite slab over the grave. Etched on the face was Jenny's name, along with her birth and death dates. Written on the front edge of the stone was, "He raiseth up the poor out of the dust." On the back we had them inscribe, "Remember the Shift Key." Though unlikely that many would understand the phrase, it had meaning to those of us who became close to Jenny, both before and after her death.

It has been many years since that Friday night. I still work in the emergency room and Karen is still home with our children. Teryl is enjoying school and Kelsi is about the same age I was when I first met Jenny. In many regards, things are much the same, but in the important areas, things have improved.

We still visit Jenny's grave every Easter. The children each place a colored egg at the base of her headstone. I contemplate the inscription on the back. Along with reading the Easter story from the Bible on Easter morning, we recount the miracle we were allowed to share with Jenny.

Our family Bible is the one that belonged to Jenny and her journal sits on the bookshelf in our front room. They act as frequent reminders of the Easter we shared with her. Because of them, we remember the true meaning of Easter throughout the year, not just in the springtime.

I do not know exactly why I forgot about Jenny after Junior High School, but I do know I will never forget our last meeting and the things that followed. That shift changed my life.

It changed many lives.